Going Quackers

by Bonnie Worth

illustrated by Ted Enik

based on the character Babe created by Dick King-Smith

A STEPPING STONE BOOK™

Random House 🏠 New York

W9-ART-415

Copyright © 1999 by Universal Studios Publishing Rights, a division of Universal Studios Licensing, Inc. Babe, Babe: The Sheep Pig, and related characters are copyrights and trademarks of Universal City Studios, Inc. All rights reserved under International and Pan-American Copyright Conventions. Published in the United States by Random House, Inc., New York, and simultaneously in Canada by Random House of Canada Limited, Toronto.

Library of Congress Cataloging-in-Publication Data
Worth, Bonnie.
Babe: going quackers / by Bonnie Worth ; illustrated by Ted Enik ; based on the character Babe created by Dick King-Smith.
p. cm.
"A Stepping Stone book."
SUMMARY: While Babe the pig is babysitting a batch of duck eggs by sitting on them, they hatch and he becomes the mother of the new ducklings, naming them, teaching them how to behave, and using them to herd his sheep.
ISBN 0-679-89468-3 (trade) — ISBN 0-679-99468-8 (lib. bdg.)
[1. Pigs—Fiction. 2. Ducks—Fiction. 3. Domestic animals—Fiction.]
I. Enik, Ted, ill. II. King-Smith, Dick. III. Title. PZ7.W88784Baae 1999
[E]—dc21 98-41325

www.universalstudios.com
www.randomhouse.com/kids

Printed in the United States of America 10 9 8 7 6 5 4 3 2 1

A STEPPING STONE BOOK is a trademark of Random House, Inc.

Contents

1
DUCK for a Day

Lula the duck wanted a vacation.

She wanted to visit her friends.

She wanted to sleep all morning. She wanted to swim all afternoon.

She wanted to fly all night.

But Lula had a nest of eggs to sit on. She could leave the nest only for a little while.

What she needed was a good egg-sitter!

First she asked the geese if they could help. But they were too busy.

Then she asked Ferdinand the duck. He wouldn't egg-sit either.

So Lula went and asked the chickens if they could help.

But none of them would egg-sit for her, either.

7

Duchess the cat slinked by. She told Lula to talk to Babe.

So Lula went and asked Babe if
he would egg-sit for her.
Of course he would!

Lula led Babe back to her nest. There were ten big eggs in it. Each egg was white with brown spots.

Babe sat down on the eggs. He was very, *very* careful.

The eggs did not break.

The eggs did not move.

The eggs did not make a peep.

Babe was happy.

2
Little Quackers

Babe sat on the eggs all day.
He talked to the eggs.
He sang to the eggs.
He hummed to the eggs.
The eggs did not break.
The eggs did not move.
The eggs did not make a peep.
Babe was happy. Until…

Crack! *Crack!* *Crack!* *Crack!*

One egg cracked open.

Two more eggs cracked open.

Three more eggs cracked open.

Another three eggs cracked open.

The very last egg cracked open.

Ten small yellow bills poked out.

Ten pairs of shiny black eyes looked around.

Ten small yellow bodies rolled out.

Ten pairs of orange webbed feet came last.

Babe was amazed!

18

The ducklings shook their little bodies.

They flapped their little wings.

They looked at Babe with their shiny black eyes.

Then they opened up their little beaks and spoke. They thought Babe was their mother!

Babe told the ducklings again and again that he was *not* their mother.

They did not listen.

He told them again and again that their real mother was coming back *very* soon.

The ducklings still did not listen.

Babe told the ducklings again and again that he did not know *anything* about ducks.

The ducklings didn't care.

They loved Babe!

Babe didn't know what to do.

Just then, Lula flew in.
Babe jumped for joy.
Now everything would be okay!

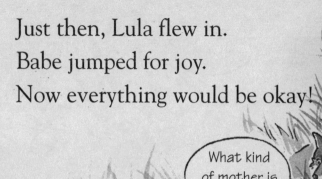

3
Mama Babe

Lula gave Babe some tips on what to teach ducklings.

1. Waddle in a line.
2. Paddle in the pond.

Then Lula flew off.

Babe was alone with the ten ducklings.

Now Babe didn't know what to do.

He thought hard.

What was the first thing parents did?

Babe knew! Parents name their kids!

But how did they do it?

Babe looked at the ducklings very closely.

Every duckling was different.

Babe smiled.

He knew just what to do.

He started naming the ducklings one by one.

Babe looked at the last little duckling. She was the littlest duckling of them all.

Babe decided to start teaching the ducklings how to waddle in a line.

First Babe waddled.

The ducklings waddled after him.

But they weren't in a line, and Tipper kept tipping over.

Babe stopped waddling.

The ducklings stopped waddling.

Babe carefully put all his ducks in a row: Quacker, Quicker, Tipper, Flapper, Tripper, Napper, Looker, Hopper, Topper, and Tiny.

This is nuts.

Mama!

He went to the front of the line and began to waddle. The ducks followed him—one, two, three, four, five, six, seven, eight, nine, ten.

They were waddling in a line!

The next duck lesson was paddling in the pond.

Babe led the ducklings to the pond.

SPLASH! Into the pond went Babe. His feet sank into the mud. Babe stopped where he was. He didn't want to go any deeper.

Then—*splish, splosh, splash, plop.* The ducklings slipped into the water one by one.

Not one little quacker sank.

They swam like ducks!

Babe was very proud.

4

Pride and Joy

The days flew by.

Quacker, Quicker, Tipper, Flapper, Tripper, Napper, Looker, Hopper, Topper, and Tiny went everywhere with Babe.

They waddled in a line.

They swam.

Babe was happy.

Babe showed off his little quackers to all the animals.

Farmer Hoggett saw Babe and
the ducklings. He missed Babe.

Mrs. Hoggett saw Babe, too. "First that pig thought he was a dog," she said. "Now he thinks he's a duck."

41

One day, Babe was sitting in the pond. He looked up at the field.

He saw Farmer Hoggett and Fly herding the sheep.

Babe missed herding sheep.

But how could he herd and take care of his little quackers at the same time?

Babe had an idea!
Babe led the ducklings to the field.

The ducklings watched Babe very carefully.

They watched him talk nicely to the sheep. They watched the sheep listen.

The sheep walked in a line. Then the sheep made a circle.

Whatever Babe asked the sheep to do, the sheep did.

And Babe was always nice and polite. He always said "Please." He always said "Thank you."

Let us try, Mama!

Babe let the ducklings herd the sheep, too. They had learned well.

They talked nicely to the sheep.

The sheep walked in a line. Then the sheep made a circle.

Whatever Quacker, Quicker, Tipper, Flapper, Tripper, Napper, Looker, Hopper, Topper, or Tiny asked the sheep to do, the sheep did.

And they were always nice and polite. They always said "Please" and "Thank you."

Babe was very, *very* proud.

And so was Farmer Hoggett.

"Sheep-pig ducks?" said Mrs. Hoggett. "What's the world coming to?"

After that, Babe and his little quackers herded the sheep up to the field every morning.

And every night, they herded them back to the fold.

Farmer Hoggett watched in wonder.

5
Up, Up, and Away!

One morning, Babe and the ducklings were up in the field.

Quack! Quack! Quack!

A noise came from the sky.

The ducklings looked up.

Look, Mama!

The very next day, the ducklings began flying lessons.

They practiced running.

They practiced jumping.

They practiced flapping their wings.

One day, as they were practic-
ing, some other ducks flew by.

Babe didn't want his little quackers to go.

But then he thought of the long, cold winter. How would he keep them warm?

He thought of what he had taught the little quackers. They could waddle in a line. They could swim. They could herd. And now they could fly.

His little quackers were not so little anymore. They were ready to leave home.

Babe was sad. But he knew what was best.

Babe kissed his little quackers good-bye.

The ducklings wanted to know if he could come, too.

Babe smiled. He looked up at his little quackers as they flew away. He was going to miss them a lot.

But he knew that the time would fly!